THE LOST WORLD
JURASSIC PARK

THE JUNIOR NOVELIZATION

THE JUNIOR NOVELIZATION

By **Gail Herman**

Based on the
motion picture screenplay
by **David Koepp**
and the novel
THE LOST WORLD
by **Michael Crichton**

GROSSET & DUNLAP • NEW YORK

Prologue

Site B:
An island off the coast of South America

The sun shone brightly on the tropical beach. Gentle waves lapped the shore. The white sand glittered. Beyond lay the jungle. Dark. Mysterious.

"*Caw! Caw!*" shrieked a bird.

And then there was silence.

The island seemed deserted when the yacht

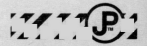

dropped anchor. A small boat ferried a mother, father, and little girl to the beach. It was so peaceful. So quiet. The perfect place for a picnic.

While her parents rested in the sun, Cathy wandered down the shore. She rounded a curve in the beach. And disappeared from her parents' view.

Cathy kicked a pebble. It landed near the thick jungle trees. *Swish, swish*. Cathy heard leaves rustle, then grow still.

Curious, Cathy edged closer to the tree line. She shaded her eyes from the sun. Was somebody—or something—in there?

Swish, swish. Suddenly a small lizard-like animal scampered out of the bush. Cathy stared. She'd never seen anything like it. Brown stripes lined its dark green body. It stood on its back legs, balancing on a thick tail. It bobbed its head like a chicken.

Then it took a step toward Cathy.

Cathy bent closer. She looked the animal in the eye. "What are you?" she asked softly. "A little bird?"

She dug into her pocket and took out a sandwich. "How 'bout some roast beef?" she said, holding it out.

The animal stretched its neck. It opened its jaws. Snap! It ripped off a mouthful of meat.

Cathy grinned. "Mom! Dad!" she called, turning her head. "You've got to see this!"

Then Cathy turned back—and gasped. Thirty more creatures were standing there. All bobbing their heads. All staring.

Cathy's smile vanished.

The animals formed a circle. They surrounded Cathy.

"Wh-wh-what do you guys want?" she stammered.

Seconds later, back at the picnic area, a shrill scream pierced the silence.

"Cathy!" The father dropped his book. The mother leaped to her feet.

They raced up the beach. They heard loud chirping. And more screams.

Frantic, they rounded the bend at breakneck speed. They caught sight of Cathy...of the strange little animals. And they stopped dead in their tracks.

CHAPTER 1

A group of business people sat at a long table. Peter Ludlow stood at the head, tapping his toe nervously.

Ludlow headed the InGen Corporation, along with his uncle John Hammond. Hundreds of workers reported to him. But Ludlow answered to the people at the table. They were InGen's board of directors, and they controlled the corporation's money. And to Ludlow, money was everything.

"Gentlemen, thank you for coming so quickly,"

Ludlow said. He opened a file and pulled out a stack of black-and-white photos. Then he tossed them onto the table.

The business people closed their eyes in horror.

"These photos were taken in a hospital in Costa Rica, South America, forty-eight hours ago," Ludlow explained. "After a family on a cruise stumbled onto Site B.

"The girl will be fine," he added. "But her parents are angry. And rich. They want to take us to court. And as you know, it will cost a lot of money to keep them quiet."

Ludlow sighed. The InGen Corporation had already spent millions of dollars in court. Lawsuits for death. For injury. All because of his uncle, John Hammond—and Jurassic Park.

It happened four years ago. John Hammond had tried to open a park. A theme park with real live dinosaurs on an island near Costa Rica, not far from Site B. But it had turned into a catastrophe. Some people got hurt. Some people died.

But, Ludlow thought, it doesn't all have to be for nothing. We can make money on this thing yet.

"This madness must stop!" he told the business people. "You've been watching the price of InGen stock fall for years. But all along we've had the very product that could bring us enormous profit.

"John Hammond wants to leave Site B alone," he told them. "He wants to let Mother Nature take her course. But I don't work for Mother Nature. I work for *you*. I think John Hammond should be kicked out of his office. All those in favor, raise your hand."

Every hand in the room went up.

The next day, in New York City, Dr. Ian Malcolm waited for a train. Tall, thin, dressed all in black, he towered over everyone else in the subway station.

Ian ducked his head, hoping no one would recognize him.

Still, a man sidled over. "You're him," he said knowingly. "The scientist on TV. The one who talked about real live dinosaurs."

Ian ignored him. But the man wouldn't go

away. *"Roar!"* he bellowed. "Is that how they sound?"

Ian shut his eyes. He felt tired. Weary of these people. Of trying to explain what really happened at Jurassic Park. And of the InGen Corporation trying to make him sound like a madman.

Everywhere he turned, people hounded him. But nobody believed him. And now, John Hammond wanted to see him. Why couldn't he just forget the whole thing?

Ian boarded a train, and a little later found himself at the door of Mr. Hammond's penthouse apartment. A butler showed him into the wealthy man's room.

Mr. Hammond lay in bed. Tubes ran from his arms to hospital machines lining the walls. He seemed older than Ian remembered. More frail.

"It's good to see you," Mr. Hammond said, smiling.

Ian grinned back. How could he not? Mr. Hammond looked so sick, he felt sorry for him. "What did you want to see me about, John?" he asked. "Your message said it was important."

"I want to apologize," Mr. Hammond replied.

"You were right about Jurassic Park. I was wrong."

Ian nodded. He'd been against it from the start.

"Instead of observing the animals," Mr. Hammond went on, "I tried to contol them. I tried to keep them caged. So we really knew nothing about them. About their behavior in the wild." He paused. "Thank goodness there's still Site B."

"Site B?" Ian repeated.

Mr. Hammond nodded. "Jurassic Park was for tourists. It was a showroom, that's all. We bred the animals on another island. Site B. We destroyed Jurassic Park. But Site B still exists."

Another island filled with dinosaurs? Ian shook his head as the nightmare flooded back. Tyrannosaurs stomping on vehicles. Snapping at people's limbs. Bloodthirsty Velociraptors, clawing...slashing...

"Unfortunately, a hurricane wiped out our factory on Site B," Mr. Hammond explained. "We had to leave the island and let the animals go in the wild. Free to grow and reproduce on their own."

"No, no, no," Ian moaned softly.

"Now there are dozens of species living together. Ruling their own little world. And I'm fighting to keep it that way. Free of human interference."

"Then you've finally done something right!" Ian exclaimed. "That island has to be left completely alone."

Mr. Hammond struggled to his feet. He shuffled to a desk and rifled through some papers until he found a yellow file. "Actually, I'm sending a team of researchers there to document the dinosaurs—and make the most amazing living fossil record the world has ever seen."

"No!" Ian burst out. "You can't send people there! Haven't you learned anything?"

Quickly, Mr. Hammond explained about Peter Ludlow's taking control of InGen—he had watched the whole board meeting from a monitor in his room—and of Ludlow's plan to take the animals away from their lost world.

"I need to build support," Mr. Hammond told Ian. "I need people behind me, wanting to keep the island the way it is. And to get that? I need proof. Photos. Videos of the animals—alive in nature."

"You must be crazy!" Ian cried. "Who are the lunatics you've found to do this for you?"

Mr. Hammond ticked off the names. "Nick van Owen, a video expert. Eddie Carr, a field equipment specialist." He took a breath. "We also have a paleontologist. An expert on animal behavior. And I was hoping *you* would be the fourth."

"Who? Me?" Ian gasped. "Of course I won't go. And furthermore, I'm going to contact the other three members and stop *them* from going."

Ian reached for the file. "What's the name of the paleontologist, anyway?"

Hammond looked away guiltily. "She came to me, Ian," he said. "She's the best in her field, after all. Her work on dinosaur families—"

Suddenly, Ian's heart began to pound. "Not Sarah!" he cried. "You mean you were going to send my girlfriend to that place?"

"No," Mr. Hammond said softly. "I mean she's already there. She insisted on making the first expedition on her own."

Ian began to pace frantically. Then he made a decision. "This is not a research mission, anymore," he said, glaring. "It's a rescue mission. It's leaving tonight. And I'm going with it."

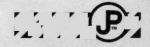

On the other side of the world, in a cafe in central Africa, Roland Tembo sat quietly reading a book. He was an older man, with the diamond-hard look of a big-game hunter.

Suddenly, Roland stopped reading. He sniffed the air. "Ajay?" he said, not turning around.

A wiry man stepped out from behind him.

"How did you know?" Ajay asked, amazed.

Roland tapped his nose. "That cheap after-shave I always send you for Christmas." He waved at a chair. "Sit down! What brings you here?"

"I got a call about an expedition to a tropical island somewhere near Costa Rica," Ajay said.

Roland sighed. He was bored with hunting—even with his good friend Ajay. They were too successful. Too good. There was no sport in it anymore.

"What quarry could possibly interest me?" he asked.

Ajay just smiled.

CHAPTER 2

It was nighttime. But a large warehouse on an empty street hummed with activity. Workers huddled over AAV's—all-activity vehicles that could cover any ground. They tinkered with engines and tested the bodies for strength.

Eddie Carr watched a metal structure rise into the air. It was a high hide—a place from which the research team would observe the animals. The equipment specialist nodded.

"It's just the right height," Ian said, walking

over, "for biting." He turned off the satellite phone he was holding. He'd been trying to reach Sarah on the island. So far, no luck.

"What's the matter with this thing?" Ian shook the phone in frustration.

Eddie sighed. "Who knows? It hasn't been field-tested yet. Nothing has. I thought we had more time. But you know you're rushing things, Doc."

Rushing things? When Sarah's life was at stake? Ian didn't think so. Not bothering to answer Eddie, he turned to Nick van Owen.

"What's your background?" Ian asked the good-looking young man unloading camera equipment.

"Wildlife. Combat. You name it," Nick told him, grinning. "I also do volunteer work for the environment.

"But this time," he added, "I'm doing it purely for the money. Mr. Hammond's paying me a lot to go along on this wild-goose chase."

Nick spoke lightly. Like he didn't believe there'd really be any dinosaurs—or any danger. Ian was about to tell him all about it...the dinosaurs...the risk...when a voice stopped him.

"Hi, Dad."

Twelve-year-old Kelly Malcolm looked around the warehouse curiously. She had dark skin like her mom, an African-American, and Ian's questioning eyes.

Now Kelly's eyes were turned to Ian. She knew why he'd asked her to come. He was going away. Again. And he wanted to say good-bye.

Ever since her mom and Ian split, Kelly had been traveling between the two. Sometimes she felt like an extra piece of luggage.

No use beating around the bush, she thought, as Ian led her away from the others so they could talk in private. "Do I have to stay with a baby-sitter again, Dad?" she blurted. "Can't I stay with Sarah while you're gone?"

"Sarah is—" Ian paused, uncertain what to say. "You're staying with a baby-sitter," he told her. "Besides, it's only for a few days."

"Then why not let me come with you?" Kelly asked hopefully. "I could be your research assistant. Like I was in Austin."

"This is nothing like Austin," Ian said, frowning.

Kelly shook her head. "You like to have kids.

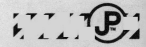

You just don't like to be with them." She sighed.

Ian's face turned red. "Hey, *I'm* not the one who split for Paris! So don't take it out on me!" he blurted. But as soon as it was out of his mouth, he wished he could take it back. He knew the words about her mother hurt Kelly as much as they hurt him.

"Dr. Malcolm!" Eddie shouted from across the warehouse. "Ready!"

Ian bent down close to his daughter. "I'm sorry, Kelly. Don't listen to me. Now I have to go. And I have to go alone." He kissed her on the cheek. "I love you."

Kelly watched as Ian walked off toward Eddie and Nick. She knew that was her cue to leave.

Then she noticed the two long trailers. They were connected by an accordion passageway kind of like a Slinky. Like two subway cars hooked together.

Dad will be traveling in these, Kelly thought.

She walked around and peered in the windows. Computers and lab equipment lined the walls—along with a large map of the Pacific Ocean. A group of islands was circled with heavy black ink. Kelly glanced around to make sure no one was looking. Then she opened the trailer door. And she slipped inside.

The next morning at dawn, Ian stood at the railing of an ocean barge. The ship rocked back and forth, crammed with equipment and supplies.

Mist sprayed Ian's face. Waves pounded the barge. Eddie leaned over the railing, looking green. "Couldn't we have just taken a helicopter?" he moaned.

"No," Ian answered. "Helicopters would disturb the animals too much. If Sarah's in trouble, I don't want to cause a stampede."

Just then, sheer cliffs broke through the fog and mist. The island, Site B, was up ahead. Sarah was there, somewhere. She has to be okay, Ian told himself. She has to!

Nick stepped close to Ian. For the first time he looked concerned. "The captain says he will drop us off onshore. But then he's heading back out.

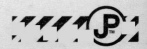

He wants to anchor a few miles offshore. We can call him by radio. But he doesn't want to hang around. He's heard too many stories."

"Stories?" Ian repeated.

"About fishermen," Nick explained. "Fishermen who came too close to the island. And never returned."

CHAPTER 3

A few hours later, the double trailers pulled up to a grassy plain at the edge of the island. Ian peered out the window. A long valley shimmered before them. Dark, thick jungle bordered both sides.

"You just don't appreciate fences until they're gone," he muttered, remembering Jurassic Park.

A satellite dish opened on the trailer roof with a soft electric hum.

"Radar," Eddie explained. He clicked a handheld monitor. "It will give us an electronic map of the island."

Ian watched the tiny screen fill with lines and colors. A red *X* appeared in the corner. "That's us," Eddie said. "And I built a finder device into Sarah's satellite phone. We should be getting a readout...."

A red triangle came onscreen. It was only a short distance from the *X*. Eddie grinned. "See, Doc? There's our girl!"

"Her *phone* is safe," Ian shot back sarcastically. "I'm so relieved. Have you got a rifle?"

Eddie nodded and slung a weapon over his shoulder. "Just about the most powerful tranquilizer gun ever made," he said proudly.

"Then let's go," Ian snapped. "And the second we get her, we are out of here!"

Nick patted his video camera. "Speak for yourself." He popped a stick of gum into his mouth. "John Hammond's paying me well for pictures of whatever's out there—and he's going to get his money's worth."

The three men started down a jungle trail. Trees and vines blocked out most of the sun. Ian checked their hand-held monitor. Little by little, the *X* was drawing closer to the triangle. Ian started to walk faster.

Finally they stepped out of the bush. They stood in a dry riverbed. Ian glanced at the screen. The *X* was right on top of the triangle.

And Sarah was nowhere to be seen.

Ian's eyes swept over the sand and dirt and trees. "Sarah should be here!" he cried.

"Over there!" Nick pointed to a battered backpack on the ground. He picked it up.

"Oh, no," Eddie exclaimed. The pack was beaten up and smeared with dirt.

Ian tore it open and pulled out Sarah's satellite phone.

"She must be nearby," Nick said, picking the backpack up and slinging it over his shoulder. "We'll split up. We'll cover more ground."

"Absolutely not!" said Ian. "We stay together. Predators look for strays that have split off from their group."

"But—" Nick began to protest. Then suddenly he wheeled around. Did those trees just move? Sway? No, he decided. It was nothing. Maybe the wind.

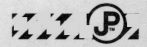

"I'll take the far edge," he continued. "Eddie, you—"

Creak! Swish! Nick stopped. That was no wind. The trees were definitely moving. Something was there.

Ian signaled them to keep quiet. Eddie readied his gun. Nick turned on his video camera.

Then something large and greenish-gray brushed by the trees right beside them. The three men jumped.

"What was it?" Ian whispered.

"Something big," Eddie hissed back.

"How big?"

"Big enough to worry about!"

Above the trees, they saw a row of plates glide by—some kind of bony armor. Nick gasped as he peered through the bush. It was a Stegosaurus!

The mighty dinosaur whipped its spiky tail back and forth as it crashed through the jungle.

A second stegosaur, about half the size of the first, lumbered behind it. A juvenile! And behind the two, came the biggest stegosaur of all.

It was a stegosaur family! Eddie couldn't help it. He burst into laughter as the animals plodded past. In a flash, Ian clapped a hand over Eddie's mouth. Then he lifted a thick blanket of leaves. There, in a large clearing, stood an entire herd of stegosaurs. All ages. All sizes.

Quickly Nick set up his equipment. Ian scanned the clearing. Still no sign of Sarah. But wait! He saw a figure, crouched behind some rocks. Yes, it was Sarah—dressed in field gear, scribbling furiously on a notepad. She turned to watch the stegosaur family, caught sight of the research team, and waved.

"She's gutsy," Nick whispered.

"She's nuts," Ian hissed.

Grinning, Sarah hurried over. "Ian!" she said breathlessly. "I'm so happy you're here!"

Then she turned back to the animals. "Can you believe this? A family group! Babies staying with their parents! I've seen nests. Eggs—"

Ian grabbed her arm, interrupting. "Are you all right? Were you attacked?"

"What do you mean?" Sarah said.

Ian held up the backpack.

"Oh, that's how it always looks," she told him. "It's my lucky pack."

She spotted one of Nick's cameras. "Hey, you don't mind if I borrow this, do you? I dropped mine in the water yesterday."

She took the camera and scrambled back into the clearing. She crept along beside the baby stegosaur, snapping shot after shot.

Nick grinned at Ian. "Should we rescue her now?" he joked. "Or after lunch?"

Whirr! Just then, the roll of film ended and the camera suddenly rewound. Startled, the stegosaurs jumped. The biggest one swung toward Sarah. Its plates bristled like a cat's fur standing on end.

Silently, Sarah began to move away.

"Sarah!" Ian shouted.

The dinosaur spun instantly toward him. Its tail whipped through the air. *Whizz!* Straight for Sarah. She leaped back, and the tail missed her by inches.

Then the animal twisted its head toward Sarah. It raised its tail, ready to strike again.

Sarah crawled like a shot into a hollow log. Safe, she thought.

Crunch! Spikes drilled through her cover, as

the creature's tail slammed down on the rotting wood. Sharp bone grazed Sarah's face.

As the dinosaur struggled to free its tail, Sarah quickly crawled out of the log. But by then the animal had lost interest. As soon as he was free, he followed the rest of the herd into the jungle. In seconds, they disappeared.

Ian, Eddie, and Nick rushed to Sarah.

"Isn't it great?" she cried.

Ian shook his head and frowned.

CHAPTER 4

Sarah followed Ian, Nick, and Eddie back to the trailers.

Nick patted his camera. "These will be incredible pictures," he told Eddie.

"Wow," was all Eddie could say.

Meanwhile, Ian had a lot he wanted to say to Sarah.

"Why didn't you tell me you were part of this?" he demanded.

"Because you would have tried to stop me," she replied. "You worry too much. You had your turn. Now it's *my* turn to see these animals first-hand. To see how they raise their young. I bet I can even prove that Tyrannosaurus rexes are loving parents, and not the vicious lizards people think they were.

"And," she went on, "I know what I'm doing. I've worked with predators for years. They stick to their game trails. If we just stay on the outer rim of the island and off the trails, the meat eaters will never bother us. We'll be fine."

Furious, Ian reeled around. "Come on, Sarah! Dinosaurs will go where there's food. They have legs, you know."

Sarah turned red. How dare he treat her like a baby. "What are you doing here, anyway?" she asked angrily. "You've never followed me any-where before."

"Hey! Someone who loves you travels thou-sands of miles to warn you. And you want to start a fight?"

Sarah's face softened. "You *love* me?"

"Didn't you know that?" Ian said softly. "Now please. You've seen dinosaurs with their young. You've got pictures to prove it. Now let's get out of here."

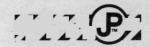

Sarah shook her head. But before she could reply, Nick bolted between them. A column of smoke rose over the trees.

"Fire!" he shouted.

The team pounded through the jungle. They burst through thick vines into the grassy plain.

In front of the trailers, a small neat campfire burned.

"We've got to put that out!" cried Sarah. "Dinosaurs can pick up scents from miles away. Different scents could bring them charging."

Nick reached for a jug of water. But Sarah grabbed his arm. "Not with that!" she said. "Water will just make more smoke. Dirt! Use dirt!"

Furiously, they kicked the ground. In seconds, the flames were smothered.

"Who started this?" Ian shouted angrily.

"It was just to make dinner," a small voice answered.

Ian spun around. Kelly stood in the trailer door.

"I wanted it ready," Kelly went on, "for when you got back."

Everyone stared, stunned. Ian tried to take it all in. His daughter...sneaking aboard the trailer...traveling all this way. And now she was on this crazy—dangerous—island!

Kelly looked at Ian's angry face. "You practically told me to come here," she said. "You said not to listen to you. I thought you were trying to tell me something."

"Kelly," Ian said. "You have no idea what's going on here."

"You're wrong, Dad." Kelly spoke quietly. "I do know. Maybe nobody else believed you about Jurassic Park. But I did."

Sarah reached out to hug her, and Ian grabbed for the satellite phone. He jabbed at the buttons trying to get a connection. He had to call the barge and get Kelly out of there now!

But nothing came through.

"Why doesn't this thing ever work?" he yelled to Eddie.

"Look, it's not like a regular phone," said Eddie. "You have to wait for a decent signal."

Disgusted, Ian took Kelly's hand and hurried to the trailer to try the radio.

"I'm taking my daughter out of here," he called over his shoulder. "Anybody coming?"

Sarah looked after him for a moment. Then she turned to Eddie. Let Ian worry, she thought. She still had work to do.

"There's a good spot for the high hide over there." She pointed to a spot near the edge of the jungle. "Those plants are poisonous. They'll keep the animals away. How tall is that thing, anyway?"

"Fifteen feet," Eddie answered.

Sarah paled. "I think I'll stick to the field," she said. "I can't stand heights. Five feet off the ground, and everything starts to spin."

Sarah strapped on her backpack. "Okay, listen up," she told Eddie and Nick. "When we're out in the field, we don't leave a scent. No bug spray. No perfume. We're here to observe. Nothing more. If we bend a blade of grass? We bend it back the way it—"

Suddenly, a low humming sound filled the air. It grew louder, until a thundering boom sounded through the jungle.

Sarah, Eddie, and Nick looked up, and Ian peered out from the door of the trailer. Three huge helicopters buzzed above them.

"It says InGen on them!" Eddie exclaimed as he watched them start to hover over a clearing in the distance. "Why would Hammond send *two* teams?"

Ian grabbed a pair of binoculars. He trained them on workers already on the ground. They were unloading huge cages. Weapons. Jeeps. Trucks.

These were not researchers. These were hunters. Out to capture prey.

"Hammond didn't send these guys," Ian said. "He did." He pointed to one person standing in the center of it all.

It was Peter Ludlow.

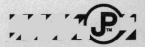

CHAPTER 5

The sun dipped below the trees as dusk fell over the jungle. A herd of peaceful dinosaurs grazed on a plain.

Suddenly, the quiet was shattered. Truck after truck tore through the bush. Engines roared. Hunters shouted.

One truck broke into the clearing, then another, and another. The dinosaurs fled across the grass. And the hunters gave chase.

As the herding trucks began their roundup,

another heavier vehicle rode onto the scene.

"We'll set up base camp here," Ludlow called into a walkie-talkie. "Over." He was sitting in the backseat, dressed in expensive safari gear.

"Cancel that order!" said a voice from up front. Roland Tembo turned around. "This is a game trail, Mr. Ludlow. Meat eaters—carnivores— hunt here. Do you want to set up camp or a dinner table?"

Ludlow reddened. "Find a new spot," he muttered into the radio.

Roland leaned back, closer to Ludlow. "Let's not forget, *I'm* in charge on this little camping trip. Your job is to sign the checks. But I don't want money. All I want is the right to hunt a tyrannosaur."

"That's fine," Ludlow said quickly.

Grinning, Roland stood in his seat and hoisted himself up on top of the truck. From there he could see the entire hunt.

Roland watched the herd of herbivores race ahead and felt his pulse quicken. He waved to the truck behind them. It was the snagger truck, designed to catch large animals without harm-

ing them. Another hunter, Dieter Stark, rode in the snagger seat, holding a long pole. A noose dangled off the end.

"Faster!" Stark shouted to Carter, the driver.

"Cycle," Roland spoke into the walkie-talkie, "break a stray from the herd. Snagger, stay ready. It will be the..." Roland stopped. He tried to remember the dinosaur's name. "The pacha...the pachyse...oh, the fat head with the bald spot!"

As the herd twisted and turned, a motorcycle zoomed along one side, cutting off their escape.

From the dense jungle on the left, two enormous heads rose up in alarm. Apatosaurs. Startled, they lumbered into the field. But the herd of pachycephalosaurs never broke stride. Instead, they raced through the apatosaurs' tree-trunk-sized legs. The motorcycle skidded, darting this way and that to keep up.

Then the biker cut off one small pachysaur. A juvenile. And the truck stopped. A hunter balanced on the back, next to a device that looked like giant padded scissors.

The hunter aimed his rifle. *Whizz!* A tranquilizer dart whooshed through the air. It hit the

pachysaur in the neck. Then Dieter Stark low-
ered his noose. He reeled the dinosaur into the
truck, like a fish on a line.

The giant scissor arms closed, holding the
pachysaur in place, and the truck rolled forward
to drop the squirming dinosaur into a waiting
cage.

"Amazing," whispered Dr. Robert Burke, one
of Ludlow's paleontologists. "A real Pachycephalosaurus."

Dieter Stark grinned. "Next!" he shouted.

Up on a ridge, a short distance away, Ian and
the others watched the hunters.

"They must not know," Sarah muttered.

Ian turned to her. "Know what?"

"They think they're in herbivore—plant-eater—
territory. But they're on a game trail." She
paused a moment. "And that's no-man's-land."

An hour later, the hunters took a break. Stark
gulped from a canteen. Water dripped down his
chin, forming a puddle at his feet.

A small, strange creature hopped over. Striped

and birdlike, it was the same dinosaur who'd come up to the little girl on the beach. It lapped at the water.

"A Compsognathus!" exclaimed Burke, who was standing with the hunters.

"Is it dangerous?" Stark asked.

"I don't think so," Burke replied. "Compys are thought to be scavengers—feeding on dead or wounded animals. And since it's never seen a human, it has no reason to fear us."

Stark pulled out a long steel rod. He touched it to the animal, and a blue electrical spark shot out. The shock sent the animal tumbling head over heels back into the bushes.

"Now it does," said Stark, chuckling.

A few yards away, Roland crouched next to an enormous footprint. He stared at the deep, three-toed print.

It could only belong to one creature. A Tyrannosaurus rex.

Ajay hurried over to study the trail. He pointed to a path in the jungle. Roland nodded, reaching for his gun.

"Hey, where do you think you're going?" called Ludlow, pulling up in his jeep.

"To collect my fee," said Roland.

The hunters took off through the bush. Gliding silently, they stepped over roots and around trees. Ajay froze at a small clearing. Ahead, a group of caves was carved into a cliff.

Roland and Ajay edged closer to the first cave. A dirt ridge protected the entrance. They saw only blackness beyond.

Roland waved Ajay forward. Carefully, they stepped around the skull of a large animal lying on the ground, then bones and more bones, and the leg of some poor creature, swarming with maggots and flies.

"This is it," Roland whispered to Ajay. "The T-rex nest."

"Eee-eee!" A squeaking sound floated out of the cave. Roland and Ajay edged up the rise of dirt, then looked down.

Inside the dark cave, a wall of dried mud rose up before them. Beyond it, a baby Tyrannosaurus rex was chewing on a bone. It stood on two legs, about four feet tall. It raised its large, wobbly head for a moment, then bent back down to finish its meal.

It was then that the rotten odor of the cave

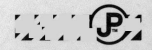

filled the hunters' nostrils. Roland held a handkerchief to his nose. "Infant's probably a few weeks old," he whispered. "Never been out of the nest. Parents won't leave it for long."

"Should we wait here for them to return?" Ajay asked.

Roland shook his head. "They'll catch our scent and know we're here before we have a chance. The trick is to get them to come to *us*."

"*Eee-eee*," the baby squealed as it took another hungry, awkward bite of flesh.

Roland stared at the infant. He had an idea.

CHAPTER 6

Darkness was falling fast. In one corner of the jungle interior, the hunters had trampled down grass and plants and set up camp.

Soon blue laser fences circled the group of tents. A large campfire roared in the center. Jeeps and trucks lined one side of the camp. Dinosaurs paced in giant cages along the other.

Ian and the others still stood on the ridge, gazing down.

"Compy, Triceratops, Pachycephalosaurus... looks like they went for herbivores or small scav-

scavengers only," Sarah noted. Then she took a step back, dizzy from the height.

"Do they really want to build a park here?" Kelly asked. "After what happened at the other one?"

"They're not building anything," Ian told her. "They're taking the animals away. Back to the mainland."

Nick grinned. "Good thing we have a backup plan. A way to stop these guys."

"A backup?" Sarah echoed.

"Yeah." Nick pulled out sharp tools. A hunting knife. A crowbar. "Me!"

But getting involved with Peter Ludlow was the last thing on Ian's mind.

"Sarah," he pleaded. "I have to get Kelly off this island now. So I'll ask you one more time. Are you coming with us?"

Sarah looked from Ian to Nick, then back to Ian. "I waited a lifetime for this," she said softly. "I won't let them take it away."

Then she nodded to Nick. And they scrambled down the hill.

In the thick of the jungle, Roland chained the baby rex to a stake in the ground. Ludlow drifted over, curious.

"Bait," Roland explained.

Ludlow snickered. "You're kidding, right? A rex doesn't care about its young. It cares about one thing. Filling its own belly."

He bent down close to the infant. He had a much better use in mind for such a creature. "The entire world will pay to watch you grow up," he told it. "You're a billion-dollar—"

Then with a sudden *whoosh!*, another small animal scurried out of the bush. Frightened, Ludlow spun around.

"Oh!" he cried, losing his balance. Then, *thud!* His feet came down on the baby rex's leg.

"*Eeehhh!*" The infant howled in pain.

Roland examined the baby, then glared at Ludlow. "You've broken its leg!" he roared.

Sarah and Nick crept to the edge of the hunters' camp. They watched as Ludlow returned, scowling, to the circle of tents. Then he

saw a satellite dish set up outside the main tent and began to grin.

They must be ready to send some kind of broadcast, Sarah thought, as several workers and hunters hurried to join Ludlow.

Sarah and Nick exchanged looks. This was their chance, while everyone was busy.

Nick gave Sarah a boost and she hurled herself over the blue lines of the electrical fence. Nick took a running start. Then he flung himself over like an Olympic vaulter.

They were inside the camp.

Slowly, quietly, they made their way to the row of trucks. Nick drew out his bolt cutter. Then he ducked underneath the first one.

Snip, snip. He cut the fuel line. Gas poured into the dirt.

Keeping watch, Sarah signaled him to go on. Nick crawled to the next truck, then the one after that. A few minutes later, Nick was done. These vehicles were not going anywhere now.

Sarah glanced around. Everyone was still in the main tent. Inside, Ludlow was speaking into a satellite phone. A camera whirred, sending his picture back to the InGen office. A screen showed the InGen business people, sitting at a table.

Perfect, thought Sarah. She and Nick made their way across the camp to the row of cages. They stopped in front of a huge, restless Triceratops, just as Ludlow was beginning his speech.

"InGen is looking for more investors," Ludlow said, "for our new waterfront theme park in San Diego, California. The complex is nearly finished." Ludlow pointed to a compy in a cage a few feet away. "And soon we will be ready, too."

Smiling, Ludlow moved to a miniature model of the park. Little toy dinosaurs stood chained in tiny cages.

"Gentlemen," Ludlow continued, "our animals are fully grown—and fully—"

Suddenly a low rumbling echoed through the tent. *Thud. Thud.* The toy dinosaurs began to shake.

Ludlow turned around. What could it be?

Then all at once, the Triceratops burst into the tent, horns ripping through the canvas walls. It tossed its head angrily from side to side. *Bang! Boom!* Lights and equipment fell to the ground, knocked over by its immense, bony frill.

The hunters cried out in surprise—and terror— as the Triceratops bellowed. Confused, it stomped across the floor. The crowd scattered as the tent toppled over and the trike dragged it through the camp.

"ROAR!" it cried, stomping through the campfire. The fabric of the tent sizzled, then caught fire. The panicked Triceratops lashed out in all directions, slicing through tent after tent. Plowing through supplies. Setting everything ablaze. The fire reached a stream of gasoline running from one of the trucks' broken fuel lines, and the flame shot up the ribbon of gas until...*Boom!* The truck exploded.

Finally, it knocked over the laser fence controls. The glowing, humming fences disappeared.

Meanwhile, out in the jungle, waiting for his prey to take its bait, Roland heard the commotion. He left the baby T-rex and raced back to camp. Black smoke filled the air. Dinosaurs roamed the grounds. The place was in ruins.

Ludlow staggered up to him. "What's going on?" Roland demanded.

Then he bent down and picked up a lock from one of the cages. It was snipped in half.

"I see we're not alone," he said.

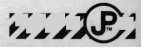

CHAPTER 7

Nick crawled out of the ruined campsite. He looked around for Sarah, but he didn't see her. He had to find their AAV...had to find Sarah. They had to get out of there now!

"*Eeee-eeee!*" Suddenly Nick skidded to a stop. There, right in front of him, was the baby rex, still chained to the stake. Still crying in pain.

Nick could see the infant's leg hanging at an unnatural angle. He shook his head in disgust. What had those hunters done now?

With one strong tug, he pulled the stake out of the ground.

Ten minutes later, Sarah raced into the clearing where they'd left their AAV. "Nick!" she exclaimed. "Thank goodness you're here!" She reached for the car door.

"Wait!" Nick cried. But it was too late. The door swung open. *"Eee-eee!"* The baby lunged out and snapped at Sarah's nose.

Sarah slammed the door. "Are you out of your mind?" she shouted.

"It's hurt!" Nick ushered her into the front seat. "Quick! Get in before the hunters hear!"

Back inside the research trailer, Ian was still trying to work the radio. He hit switch after switch. The radio squawked, then salsa music piped through. Ian sighed. Another music station. Still no ship!

In the jungle a short distance away, Eddie was

setting up the high hide. Ian thought it looked like a playground jungle gym—like a caged metal platform on stilts.

The whole thing's a waste of time, Ian thought. They had to get out of this place now!

"We've got to find the right frequency," Ian told Kelly. "The right number on the dial to radio the boat."

Kelly flipped open a nearby book. Ian ran his fingers down columns of numbers. "Ah here!" he said, stopping at a listing.

Swiftly, he turned the dial. Noise...static... music...

"Almost there," he muttered. "Almost—"

Just then, Nick and Sarah flung open the door. Ian stared at the screeching infant as they carried it in.

"No lectures, Ian," Sarah begged. She opened a drawer full of medical supplies and pulled out a small syringe.

"Wow!" said Kelly.

"Hold it tight, Nick!" Sarah ordered. Quickly she injected the baby dinosaur with a tranquilizer. Then she held a small X-ray transmitter up to its leg. Its skeleton flashed on a monitor.

"It's a fracture." She pointed to a black line in the bone.

"Sarah!" Ian said angrily. "This is trouble!"

"But the baby can't walk," Sarah announced. "A broken leg means death for it. A predator could find it and pick it off in minutes."

She tossed aside medical equipment, searching for something to make a cast out of. Blood from the dinosaur wound dripped down her shirt. The infant's screams grew louder and louder.

Kelly backed away, feeling more and more nervous. All this talk of predators and death. The screaming baby. It was too much.

"Other animals are going to hear this, aren't they?" she said shakily. "I want to get out of here."

"It's okay, honey," Ian told her. "I'm calling the boat. You'll be out of here in no time."

"I mean out of this trailer," said Kelly. Her voice rose in panic. "Now!"

Ian drew in his breath. He had to do something, quickly.

The high hide.

"Eeeehhh!" the baby shrieked.

Inside the high hide, Kelly jumped. The sound traveled so far. She wondered who else had heard it.

"This is the safest place you can be," Ian assured her. "Remember what Sarah said before? With these poisonous plants all around us, the animals won't even know we're here. We're going to be fine."

"Eeehh!" the baby screamed again.

"ROARR!" Just then an answering cry thundered from the jungle.

Ian pulled Kelly close. He knew that sound. A Tyrannosaurus rex. Searching for its child. He looked down at the trailer. He had to warn Sarah and Nick.

"I have to get down," he said.

"No, Dad!" Kelly grabbed his arm. "Stay here!"

"ROAR!" came the sound out of the jungle. Louder. Closer.

"I'm coming right back," Ian promised. He looked deep into Kelly's eyes, begging her to understand.

Kelly smiled, trying to be brave.

And then Ian was gone.

Ian darted into the trailer. Sarah had just finished molding an aluminum-foil cast around the baby's leg. She used Nick's used chewing gum to keep it in place.

"Just one more injection," she told Nick. "And that should be it."

"No," Ian said. He grabbed the baby rex. "We have to get this thing out of here right now!"

"*Rroarrr!*" The tyrannosaur's deafening cries could be heard in the trailer now.

"What is *that?*" asked Sarah.

"Mommy's very angry," Ian replied.

"*Eeee-eee!*" The baby cried out as if in response.

Thud! Thud! Suddenly the whole trailer began to shake and rattle. Equipment crashed to the floor. The rex was right outside. Its head swung down and peered through the window.

Ian, Sarah, and Nick froze.

"*Grr, grr, grr,*" the rex cooed to its baby.

The sound seemed to calm the infant. "*Gr, gr,*" it gurgled back happily.

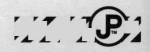

Then another tyrannosaur peeked in through the opposite window.

"Make that Mommy and Daddy," Ian muttered.

"They've come for their baby!" Sarah exclaimed.

"Well, let's not disappoint them," Ian said quickly.

Hurriedly, they carried the baby to the door. The animals followed them from window to window. Watching. Ian reached for the door handle and the door creaked open.

"*Ee-aah-ee!*" The baby squirmed free and toddled excitedly over to its parents. Ian quickly closed the door.

They heard snuffling and cooing. Then, *thud, thud, thud*. The noise grew softer as the dinosaurs moved off into the jungle.

Nick turned to Ian and Sarah, his face pale. "All right," he said. "Now do we stay? Or do we go?"

"Go!" they all said at once.

Ian reach for the radio microphone. He would make contact with the waiting ship this time....

Thud, thud.

"Ian?" Sarah whispered.

The tyrannosaurs were back.

CHAPTER 8

Boom! One dinosaur smashed into the trailer, rocking it back and forth. The other dinosaur waited a moment. Then it charged, too.

"Hang on to something!" Nick shouted.

The three people hurled themselves at the refrigerator, the table, the counter. Anything that was bolted down.

Boom! The trailer pitched onto its side. *Boom!* Another hit. It turned upside down. Ian, Sarah, and Nick dropped to the ceiling. Pots, pans, and supplies rained down on their heads.

The dinosaurs charged again, butting the trailers with their massive heads. Ian felt the trailers slide through mud. He crawled to a window.

"No!" he moaned. "They're pushing us over the cliff."

And the rexes kept pushing. Ian, Nick, and Sarah scrambled forward, toward the other end of the trailer—the one farthest from the edge. But they couldn't keep their balance. Ian fell near Sarah's backpack. He saw the satellite phone sticking out. The phone! They'd need that! Frantic, Ian lunged.

"Oh!" he cried as the trailer plunged over the cliff. It banged against rock, held in place by the connected trailer. The accordion passageway twisted and stretched.

Ian dropped the phone as he tumbled down...down. "*Oof!*" He grabbed a table leg to stop his fall.

Sarah gripped the refrigerator handle, her knuckles white with effort. But she couldn't hold on any longer. "*Ahhh!*" she screamed.

Crack! She smashed into the back windshield. Five hundred feet below, waves pounded the rocky shore. The glass quivered under her weight. Tiny lines spread quickly.

The trailer window was about to shatter.

"Oh, please," Sarah whimpered. She glanced down, and her head spun. "Oh, please."

"Hang on!" Ian called. He began to crawl closer. "Nick!" he shouted. "Get that phone!"

Nick squinted from his perch on the counter. The phone was balanced on a table leg, not far away.

Nick stretched out his hand...reaching...reaching. One finger touched the phone. Two fingers.

Then suddenly the trailer shuddered. The phone toppled down, smashing into the windshield next to Sarah. The glass splintered into dozens of pieces.

And the phone plunged into the sea.

"*Ahhhh!*" Sarah fell through open space.

Ian lunged for her. Just in time. He grabbed her hand. Sarah held it tight, dangling in midair.

Nick peered through the front windshield. He saw the dinosaurs nod to each other, as if satisfied with the damage. Then he watched them lumber away.

C-r-e-e-e-a-k! The trailer's connector stretched further. The hanging trailer jerked. Any minute now, Nick knew they'd be goners.

"Climb!" he yelled. "Fast!"

Grunting, Sarah pulled herself back into the trailer.

Outside, Eddie drove toward the cliffside at breakneck speed. He'd seen the dinosaurs from the high hide. But he could only guess what was happening. "Hang on!" he pleaded. "Hang on!"

He skidded into the clearing and caught his breath. The first trailer was about to go over! He jumped out of the AAV. In a flash, he tied a long rope around a tree.

Then he crept through the first trailer, clutching the rope. "Catch!" he shouted to Nick, tossing it down.

Now, Eddie told himself, I have to secure the trailers.

Eddie grabbed hold of the power winch on the AAV's front grill and raced back to hook it up to the dangling trailers.

Screech! The cable pulled taut and the trailers stopped.

Now to tow the helpless vehicle back to safety.

Eddie dove into the driver's seat and gunned the engine. *Roar!*

But the sound of the motor was answered by another roar in the distance.

"ROAR!"

The tyrannosaurs were back! Eddie trembled in terror. He threw himself under the steering wheel...hoping...praying...they wouldn't see him.

But it was too late.

"ROAR!" The rexes stomped closer.

And Eddie knew nothing could save him now.

In the trailer, Ian, Sarah, and Nick clung to the rope Eddie had thrown them. They heard their friend's screams. Louder and louder. Then they faded away.

Creak! The trailer dipped lower. It's over, Ian thought. The end. For Eddie and for us.

The trailers dropped and plummeted down, falling around Ian, Nick, and Sarah. But the three held tightly to the rope.

Windows flashed by...then the passageway.

And suddenly Ian, Nick, and Sarah popped out through the broken front windshield.

For a moment they dangled, nothing but air between them and the rocks below. Then hand over hand, bit by bit, they pulled themselves up the rope. The climb seemed endless.

But just when they thought they'd never make it, a hand reached down. Then another and another. The three were pulled to safety.

By Roland and the other hunters.

CHAPTER 9

The two groups stared at one another. One was there to preserve nature. The other was there to change it. But there was nothing to say, really. Nothing to do but try to find a way off this island. Together.

Ian brought Kelly down from the high hide and followed the others to the hunters' campsite. There the two teams pooled their remaining supplies. It wasn't much. Just a few bags of food. Some tents and sleeping bags. No phone. No radio. No way to call for help.

"We're stuck here," Roland said shortly. "Thanks to you people."

"Hey!" Nick exploded. "We came here to observe. You came to strip the place bare. All you care about is what you can take!"

Ian was in no mood for arguing, though. He hugged Kelly tight. Silently, he thanked Eddie for giving his life. For allowing the rest of them to live. But for how much longer?

"Listen," Sarah spoke urgently. "By taking the baby rex into our camps, we might have changed the tyrannosaurs' territory."

"Yes," Dr. Burke agreed. He nodded with a knowing air. "That must be why they destroyed the trailers. They feel like it's their territory to defend."

"That means we have to move. Right now!" Sarah told the others.

"Move where?" asked Nick. "Our boat, their air-lift—they're both waiting for orders we can't send."

Ludlow checked a map. "There's a communications center in the old worker village. It runs on natural power—heat and sun—so it should work. If we can get there, we can send a radio call for help."

"How far is it?" asked Nick.

"A day's walk," Ludlow answered. "But that's not the problem."

Roland turned to him. "What is?"

"Velociraptors."

Raptors! Ian's eyes opened wide. Carnivores. Pack hunters. Not as big as T-rexes. But strong. And smart. With razor-sharp claws on each foot that could tear a man apart.

"Our satellites show that their nesting sites are on the island's interior—near the village," Ludlow continued. "That's why we planned on keeping to the outer rim."

"The rexes will probably keep tracking us, too," added Sarah.

"I'm certain we can handle ourselves," said Dieter Stark.

"I'm certain we can't," argued Ian.

"Well, I don't see much choice," said Roland. He clapped his hands. "Saddle up, people. Let's get going."

The two groups marched through the jungle. A

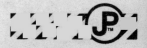

full moon rose over the trees, lighting their way. Time passed. Slowly night turned to day. The heat grew stronger. Animals hooted and hissed. And still they marched...over roots and vines...pushing aside branches and leaves.

Roland gazed around at the group. Staggering. Exhausted. "Five-minute break!" he called.

Everyone dropped to the ground. Roland leaned his gun against a tree. He went to talk to Ludlow.

Nick eyed the abandoned gun. A gun designed to kill animals already extinct. A gleam came into his eye.

Meanwhile, Dieter Stark pulled out a wad of toilet paper. "Wait here for me," he told Carter. Then he slipped off the trail...into the jungle.

He didn't notice Carter's headphones blaring music in his ears. He didn't realize Carter hadn't heard him.

Stark poked and prodded his way through the bush. Suddenly he froze. An animal scurried close. Stark recognized it. It was a compy—just like the one he zapped before.

Smiling, Stark pulled out his electrical rod.

"Don't you know it's not polite to sneak up on people?" he said.

He touched the rod to the compy's back and— *Z-z-z-!*—the animal jerked as the blue bolt of electricity danced over its body. Then, whimpering, it limped away.

Stark slid the rod back into the loop on his belt and pushed through the leaves, trying to get back to the others. "Hey, Carter?" he called. "Carter?"

But there was no answer—only more scurrying sounds. Louder. Closer. Stark began to run. But he tripped over a root and landed flat on his face. When he looked up, he saw the dinosaur he'd wounded.

And forty other compys charging right at him.

Together, they attacked.

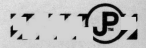

CHAPTER 10

The break was over. The two teams struggled to their feet. Roland looked around. Stark was nowhere to be seen. Roland ordered the others on. But he stayed behind, scouting the area.

Less than fifteen minutes later, the marchers arrived at a high ridge. From there they could see the other side of the island: the old worker village, their destination. Between them stood unbroken jungle.

Roland came up quietly to Sarah. "Did you find Stark?" she asked.

Roland nodded grimly. "At least the parts they didn't like," he muttered. Then he looked out over the jungle toward the village. "The operations building is down in there," he said. "The climb down won't be easy. We'll eat. Sleep. One hour. Then we'll hit it."

Some men dropped to the ground, right where they stood. Others rested against trees, and some hurriedly pitched their tents.

Inside one, Kelly and Sarah unrolled their sleeping bags and lay down while Ian went off to look around the campsite.

Yawning loudly, Sarah took off her heavy overshirt and hung it over the tent bar to air out. At first she didn't notice the bloodstain on the front, still fresh from the baby rex. Then her eyes fell on the spot. Her mouth opened in alarm.

Was it enough to attract a Tyrannosaurus rex?

Boom! The vibrating sound of heavy footsteps answered the question for her.

The rex!

Sarah snatched the shirt. She flung it to the ground. "Dig!" she told Kelly.

The two pawed furiously at the dirt, trying to make a hole in which to bury the scent.

Bmbb! BMBB! Sarah and Kelly covered over the shirt and jumped into Sarah's sleeping bag. Sarah zipped it up. Almost finished, she thought. Almost—

Then the rex poked its snout through the tent flap. It sniffed and snorted. First the spot where the shirt was buried. Then the sleeping bag. Inside, Kelly clung to Sarah, terrified.

"Roar!" The dinosaur raised its head, lifting the tent off the ground.

Those already asleep stirred at the noise, slowly at first. Then one by one they saw the T-rex. In a panic, they began to run.

"Stop!" Ian shouted. "Don't run!" Then he noticed the sleeping bag...and Kelly and Sarah squirming to get out. They were stuck. And the rex hovered inches away.

"Kelly!" Ian cried. He tried to get closer. To help. But a wall of stampeding hunters knocked him down.

Watching the whole scene from the edge of the clearing, Roland drew his gun. He would take care of this. He aimed at the dinosaur, lining up for a clean shot. He squeezed the trigger.

Click. Nothing happened.

Roland snapped open the chamber. His cartridges had been stolen!

From another part of the camp, Nick burst out of the crowd and rushed over to Sarah and Kelly. He reached into the sleeping bag and pulled them to their feet.

"ROAR!" Suddenly, the second rex thundered into camp. The hunters and Nick and Sarah and Kelly bolted the other way. But the second rex followed them into a steep, narrow valley.

Meanwhile, Roland eyed the first tyrannosaur, now bellowing angrily before him. Frantically, Roland scrambled across the ground to a box marked "Warning! Tranquilizing Nerve Agents!" and clanged it open. Clumsily, he grabbed one of three tranquilizing rifles and raised it to his shoulder.

The rex was only yards away. It swung its head and roared, ready to strike.

"Tranquilizers, please work fast," Roland muttered. And he pulled the trigger.

CHAPTER 11

The running crowd snaked through the jungle ravine. The tyrannosaur charged behind.

"Kelly!" Ian called down from the rocks above. "Get out of there! You'll be trapped!"

But the gulch was too steep. And Kelly was in the middle of the fleeing pack, running with Nick and Sarah. There was nothing she could do. She had to keep running...running...running....

The dinosaur drew closer. Carter, the driver, looked back. Panicking, he fell to the ground. He struggled to stand. But, desperate to escape, the crowd mowed him down.

"*Ahhh!*" cried Carter, as he looked up to see the dinosaur's foot coming down upon him.

Up ahead, Nick heard the cry. They could never outrun a rex. No way. Then he spotted a waterfall off to the side. Seizing hold of Sarah and Kelly, he pushed them straight through the rushing water.

They landed on a small, rocky platform, just behind the waterfall. The three crowded together. Breathless. Terrified. They heard the shouts and screams from outside.

"*Shh,*" Nick said softly. If they were quiet, the rex might pass right by.

Then—*splash!*—Dr. Burke burst noisily through the water. "Get out of the way," he shouted, elbowing Kelly to the edge of the platform. He pushed against the wall, shoving the others closer to the water...closer to the dinosaur.

Foom! The rex's head popped through the watery curtain. Its long blue tongue slithered up to the humans, trying to wrap around them.

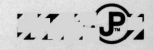

Burke pushed back even farther.

"Stop!" Sarah cried. "You're pushing Kelly out!"

But Burke didn't stop. He burrowed deeper against the wall. Until suddenly, hundreds of centipedes swarmed out of the broken rock and dropped onto his head. Instinctively, Burke cried out in surprise and leaped away—straight onto the rex's waiting tongue.

The cold, blue tongue curled around Burke. It dragged him out screaming and kicking.

"No!" he shouted again and again. And then there was silence, as the sound of the rex's heavy footsteps faded away.

Minutes later, another figure crashed through the waterfall. Ian.

He flung his arms around Kelly and Sarah.

"Thank you," he told Nick.

Free of the chasing T-rex at last, the hunters finally climbed out of the ravine. They came to a large open plain. Tall, wide grass blew in the breeze.

Ajay stopped at the edge. "No!" he shouted. "Don't go into the long grass."

But the men kept running. Ajay looked after them, uncertain. Should he follow? Try to make them turn around? Or should he find someplace safe?

Taking a deep breath, he plunged into the grass.

Farther into the grass, the men looked around. Not a dinosaur in sight. They were safe. They began to laugh.

Then they saw the grass ripple. Sway. Something was moving toward them. Quickly. Quietly.

Suddenly, one hunter was yanked to the ground. Then another was dragged below the grass.

A third hunter heard a soft rustling. He watched a long, upright tail glide toward him. Before he could make another move, the dinosaur sprang into the air and struck out with long curved claws.

Raptors, Ajay thought.

Then he saw the four torpedo tails heading straight for him. And he closed his eyes and waited.

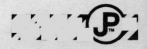

A few moments later, Ian, Kelly, Sarah, and Nick raced out of the same ravine and onto the grassy plain.

"*R-r-r-r.*" Suddenly Ian heard a familiar snarl.

"Raptors!" he cried. "Go!" he shouted to the others. "Go! As fast as you can!"

He grabbed Kelly's hand, and they all took off. A raptor leaped after them, snapping at their heels.

Faster and faster, they plunged headlong through the grass. Then the next thing they knew, the ground disappeared beneath them.

They tumbled down a steep hillside. Thorns and roots tore at their clothes. Twigs scratched their faces. Finally they landed at the bottom.

Kelly clutched Ian's arm as they staggered to their feet. A stretch of sand spread out before them like nothing they had ever seen before. Skulls, tails, bits of bones littered the ground.

Sarah gasped. "It's a dinosaur graveyard!"

Then Ian pointed to a stand of buildings in the distance. The worker village!

Nick knelt in a runner's crouch. "Every second counts," he said. "I'll run ahead to the communication center and send the radio call."

He sprinted for the village. Minutes later he was running past abandoned stores and houses, and into a small square building.

Nick scanned the room. Dust, dirt, and vines covered furniture and equipment. Then he spied the radio, built into one wall. He darted over, flipping switches quickly.

Nothing happened.

Nick sucked in his breath, desperate for the radio to work.

Finally, it began to glow green, red, and yellow.

It was at that same moment that Peter Ludlow crawled out of the muddy puddle in which he had been hiding. He tossed aside a tattered tent canvas and wiped his face.

He looked around at the demolished campsite. The ripped tents. The trampled supplies.

Then Ludlow saw something else. One of the adult T-rexes. Flat on the ground, out cold.

Ludlow crept closer. A tranquilizer dart stuck out of its neck.

And Ludlow grinned.

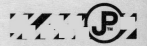

CHAPTER 12

Ian, Sarah, and Kelly limped across the sand. Bit by bit they neared the old buildings.

Then they stopped as a low roaring sound filled the air. They looked right, then left, and finally up. Ian smiled. It was a helicopter.

"Nick made it!" he shouted. He had called for help!

They all waved as Nick climbed out onto the roof of the operations building. He yelled something back to them, but his voice was drowned out by the roar of the helicopter. What was he trying to say?

"I can't hear him," Ian said. "Let's just keep going."

But just then a snarling mass of green slammed into Sarah. *"Ahh!"* she cried as the raptor took her down and sank its teeth into something soft ...a backpack!

The raptor snapped its head and ripped the bag off her back, and Sarah rolled away. Then she raced for the first building she saw.

Ian shoved Kelly after her. "Follow Sarah!" he shouted. "I'll keep this thing busy here."

At first, Kelly didn't budge. She was afraid to leave her father.

"I love you," he said softly. "Now, run!"

Kelly took a deep breath and ran.

"Yah!" Ian cried, pounding his chest. He waved his arms at the raptor. *"Yah!"* Then he charged right at it.

The raptor stood its ground. It opened its mouth wide. Quickly, Ian skidded to a stop.

"R-r-r." The raptor pounced.

Ian spun, bolting into another building. The

gas station. He slammed the door shut, just as the raptor tried to leap inside.

"*Rrr!*" The raptor sprang through a window, shattering the glass. Ian raced back outside, but so did the raptor.

Quickly Ian dove back. He took cover behind the door. Snarling, the raptor lunged.

Bang! It blasted the door from its hinges. Ian flew back, back, back—right through a window in the far wall. The door slammed against the wall. It sealed the window tight. At last, the raptor couldn't follow.

Meanwhile, Kelly and Sarah gazed around the windowless building they had found shelter in. It was really more like a shed, three stories high, filled with ladders and narrow metal walkways. Hammers and tools lined the walls.

Scratch, scratch. Kelly jumped closer to Sarah. *Hiss!* Another raptor! This one was digging a hole on the other side of the door. It was trying to get inside.

Sarah pulled Kelly to the opposite wall. They

bent low and started shoveling away dirt to make an escape tunnel.

Sarah pried off the bottom plank. She motioned to Kelly to crawl through.

Kelly crouched and began to swing her legs under. *Hiss!* A raptor claw sliced the plank. There was no getting out!

Sarah dragged Kelly back in and pulled her to her feet. They gazed up at the narrow walkways. "Can you climb?" she asked.

Kelly didn't answer. She just grabbed hold of a low bar and swung herself onto a platform. Sarah leaped after her.

Suddenly the door banged open. "Kelly?" Ian shouted, standing below.

"Up here!" Kelly cried.

Ian raced to a ladder. But just as he began to climb, a raptor jammed its head through the hole Sarah and Kelly had dug. *Crack!* The wall splintered.

Snapping its jaws, the raptor thrashed its way inside.

"Dad! Come on!" yelled Kelly.

The raptor sprang onto the scaffolding after Ian. The walkway shook with its weight.

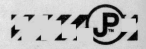

Ian slipped. He plunged toward the ground . . . past the raptor...into a maze of bars. Kelly stared down in horror. Ian was pinned.

Then the raptor jumped down. It snarled, about to strike. Kelly wiped her hands on her jeans. Then she leaped into space. Catching hold of a low bar, she twirled around it like a gymnast. Then she let go and sailed through the air.

"*R-r-r!*" The raptor readied to pounce at Ian, claws flashing. But Kelly rammed into it, feet first.

The raptor hurled through the wall of the building, screaming in pain. Kelly tumbled onto the platform next to her father. Holding hands, they jumped to the ground.

Ian looked up at Sarah, who had kept climbing to the top. "You're safer up there," he yelled to her. "Take the roof."

Then he turned back to Kelly. And together they ran out to the street.

Sarah kicked out the window at the top of the building and made her way onto the roof. At the end of the street, she saw the helicopter hovering. Only a few buildings away. But she was so high up. How was she ever going to make it?

Holding her breath, Sarah leaped over to the next building. She pulled herself to the top of its sloping roof.

Hiss! A raptor poked its head over the other side. Quickly Sarah edged back. She felt something give. The old roof was breaking apart!

Boards slid down, taking Sarah with them...taking her away from the raptor. Then she glanced down. A second raptor was waiting for her on the ground.

Sarah rolled off the sliding plank. She grabbed onto the roof edge and clung, swinging back and forth.

One raptor hissed above her.

One raptor snarled below.

Desperate, Sarah pulled off another loose shingle. She hurled it at the animal on the ground. Again and again she pried off the shingles. Suddenly, a slew of rotted roofing boards slid down.

The top raptor lost its footing and—*thud!*—fell onto the raptor below.

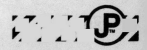

Surprised, the vicious animals snarled at each other. They slashed out, clawing and biting, forgetting about Sarah.

But Sarah couldn't hold on any longer. She groaned, dropping down onto the ground beside them. Something grabbed her and she screamed. But it was only Ian and Kelly, pulling her away.

The three raced down the street...toward the helicopter...toward safety.

It was going to be all right.

Nick slumped against the helicopter seat. He felt drained. Ian sat across from him with one arm around Kelly and the other around Sarah.

Sarah sighed with relief and peered out the window. Another helicopter was picking up more survivors. She saw Peter Ludlow, Roland, and some hunters.

Suddenly she shot forward. She'd glimpsed something out the window on the other side. Something huge.

"No!" she cried.

Everyone turned to look. Down below, workers were tying up the giant rex. Another man held the baby.

Then Sarah, Nick, and Ian gazed out to sea where a giant freight ship chugged toward the island, ready to take the dinosaurs away.

Ian's eyes gleamed with fiery determination. "Now I'm mad."

CHAPTER 13

It was nighttime in San Diego. Peter Ludlow stood on the dock of a waterfront park. A large crowd of business people gathered around him: the InGen board of directors.

Ludlow was speaking about the park he would open in a matter of days.

Ian and Sarah stepped up to the edge of the crowd. They'd come to see what Ludlow had done.

Suddenly, the harbormaster pushed through

the crowd. "The ship with the dinosaur is heading into port," he told Ludlow. "But they're coming in much too fast. And I can't contact them!"

Ludlow followed the man back to the harbormaster's shack and watched the blip on the radar screen drawing quickly closer.

"Reverse direction," the harbormaster spoke into the radio microphone. "Reverse—"

But the roar of the freighter's engine drowned out his words. The ship burst through the fog. It was going at full speed. Heading right for the park!

Screech! Metal hit concrete and wood. The ship ripped through the dock. Everyone fled in panic. They dove behind crates and under benches, as the ship crashed through wires and electrical boxes. Then everything went black.

Finally the ship groaned to a halt. Ludlow crawled out of his hiding place and climbed aboard. Ian and Sarah followed.

The ship seemed deserted. Blood streaked the deck. Giant chains lay on the ground, broken to bits.

"What happened?" yelled Ludlow. "Where's the crew?"

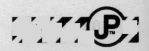

Ian tried to call him back. "We'd better get off this boat," he warned.

But Ludlow wouldn't listen. "Check the cargo hold," he ordered a guard. "Maybe the crew's hiding down there."

The guard hit a large switch, and heavy steel doors on the ship's deck began to open.

"No!" shouted Ian, just as a deafening roar swept over the ship and the tyrannosaur sprang from the hold.

"*Aaaah!*" People scattered. The rex bounded forward. But instead of attacking, it leaped off the boat as fast as it could.

Ian rushed to the railing. He saw the dinosaur break through the fences...and head into the city.

Any minute now, Sarah knew, the rex would get hungry. It would attack. They had to get it back on board the ship. They had to get it back to the island. But how?

"The baby!" Sarah cried. "We need the baby!"

Ian and Sarah hurried to a cage built under the park's amphitheater.

Inside, the baby rex was fast asleep. Ludlow had brought it back earlier with him on his plane and had injected it with tranquilizers.

Working together, Ian and Sarah loaded the infant into their car.

"Now how do we find the adult?" Sarah asked.

"Follow the screams," Ian said.

In a nearby neighborhood, the rex lumbered down a busy street. Cars swerved around it. Drivers lost control. People ran down the side-walks, screaming.

Sarah was right. It was ready to attack.

"*ROAR!*"

Frightened shouts echoed down the street. The rex swung its mighty head. It lifted up a man and prepared to chomp.

Then suddenly it sniffed. It dropped the man and sniffed again. It gazed down the street, a hopeful look on its fierce face.

One lone car zoomed closer. Inside, Ian slammed on the brakes. The car spun complete-ly around.

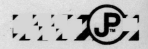

The rex lunged. Its baby was inside. But Ian hit the gas. "Back to the boat!" he shouted, tires squealing.

The rex raced after the car. It snapped at the fender. Again and again. It was gaining ground. Closing the gap. But they were almost to the dock. Almost to the boat.

Suddenly the rex reared forward, clamping down on metal and rubber. "Jump!" cried Ian.

Clutching the baby, Sarah and Ian leaped from the car.

"Hurry, hurry," Ian panted as he ran with the baby, past Peter Ludlow, to the boat. "Hurry!"

The rex dropped the car and raced after Ian and Sarah. Helicopters hummed in the sky above. They cornered the rex, searchlights glaring.

"Tell them to shoot the adult!" Ludlow ordered from the dock. "Just get me that baby back alive!"

Then he followed Ian and Sarah onto the boat. But just as his feet hit the deck, Ludlow heard a splash. He looked overboard. Ian and Sarah had jumped.

"Hey!" Ludlow yelled. "What did you do with that infant? I want that infant, you hear me!"

"*Eeee-eee.*" Ludlow heard a cry from below deck.

"Thank goodness," he muttered. The T-rex was a goner, but the baby was his!

Ludlow hurried down the steps into the ship's hold and lifted up the baby.

Thump! The boat lurched. Ludlow gazed up, surprised. Then he saw it. The adult T-rex.

The huge dinosaur bent its head, cooing softly. The baby, finally waking up from its sleep, gurgled with happiness.

Ludlow froze. Carefully he put the baby down. He backed away.

Thud! The T-rex jumped down into the hold. It towered over Ludlow.

"Wh-wh-wh-what do you want?" Ludlow stammered.

The dinosaur bumped him with its head and nudged him toward the baby. Ludlow scrambled away. But the rex knocked him to the ground. Then it nodded to its baby.

The baby leaped onto Ludlow's chest, jaws

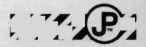

opened wide. And suddenly Ludlow understood.

It was feeding time.

From the dock, Sarah heard Ludlow cry out. She clambered up the ship's ladder. In a flash, she took it all in. Ludlow, dead. The T-rex belowdecks. Still loose. Still dangerous.

She spied Ludlow's tranquilizer gun lying on the deck. She scooped it up. Aimed.

And then she fired.

By 11 o'clock, it was all over the television news. There was a Lost World. An island filled with dinosaurs.

"A tyrannosaur and its baby were taken off an island," reporters told viewers. "But a freight ship is carrying them back as we speak."

Ian, Kelly, and Sarah watched the ship on the screen chugging down the South American coast. Exhausted, Ian and Sarah closed their eyes and began to doze.

Kelly smiled, tucking a blanket under their

chins. Everything was okay. The dinosaurs were heading home. People believed in dinosaurs now. And they also believed in her father.

"These creatures need our absence," John Hammond was saying on TV. He looked younger. Stronger. "We need to step aside. Trust in nature. Then life will find a way."

Kelly pictured the island...stegosaurs grazing...compys jumping...rexes roaring. And she smiled once more.

They would never be seen by humans again...maybe.